STONE ARCH BOOKS
a capstone imprint

STONE ARCH BOOKS™

Published in 2015
by Stone Arch Books
A Capstone Imprint
1710 Roe Crest Drive
North Mankato, MN 56003
www.capstonepub.com

Originally published by DC Comics in
the U.S. in single magazine form as Beware
the Batman #4.

DC Comics
1700 Broadway, New York, NY 10019
A Warner Bros. Entertainment Company

Cataloging-in-Publication Data is available
at the Library of Congress website:
ISBN: 978-1-4342-9741-9 (library binding)

Summary: Just when Batman is able to provide
Kirk Langstrom, a.k.a. the Man-Bat, with a cure
to his affliction, a second man-sized bat starts
terrorizing Gotham City! Can Batman count on
Kirk to help stop this shadowy new foe?

STONE ARCH BOOKS
Ashley C. Andersen Zantop *Publisher*
Michael Dahl *Editorial Director*
Sean Tulien *Editor*
Heather Kindseth *Creative Director*
Alison Thiele and Peggie Carley *Designers*
Tori Abraham *Production Specialist*

DC COMICS
Alex Antone *Original U.S. Editor*

Printed in China by Nordica.
0914/CA21401510
092014 008470NORDS15

BEWARE THE BATMAN™

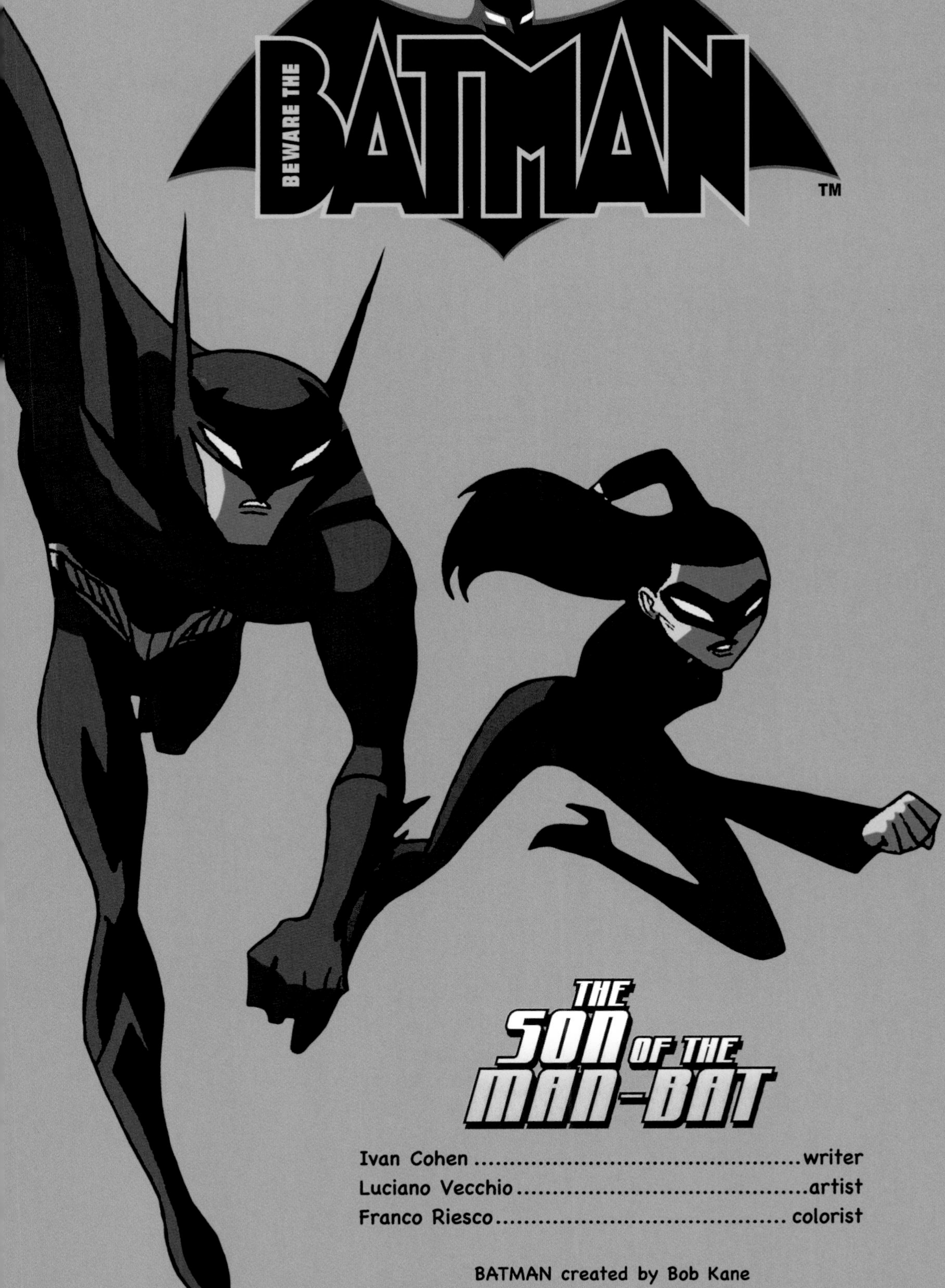

THE SON OF THE MAN-BAT

Ivan Cohen .... writer
Luciano Vecchio .... artist
Franco Riesco .... colorist

BATMAN created by Bob Kane

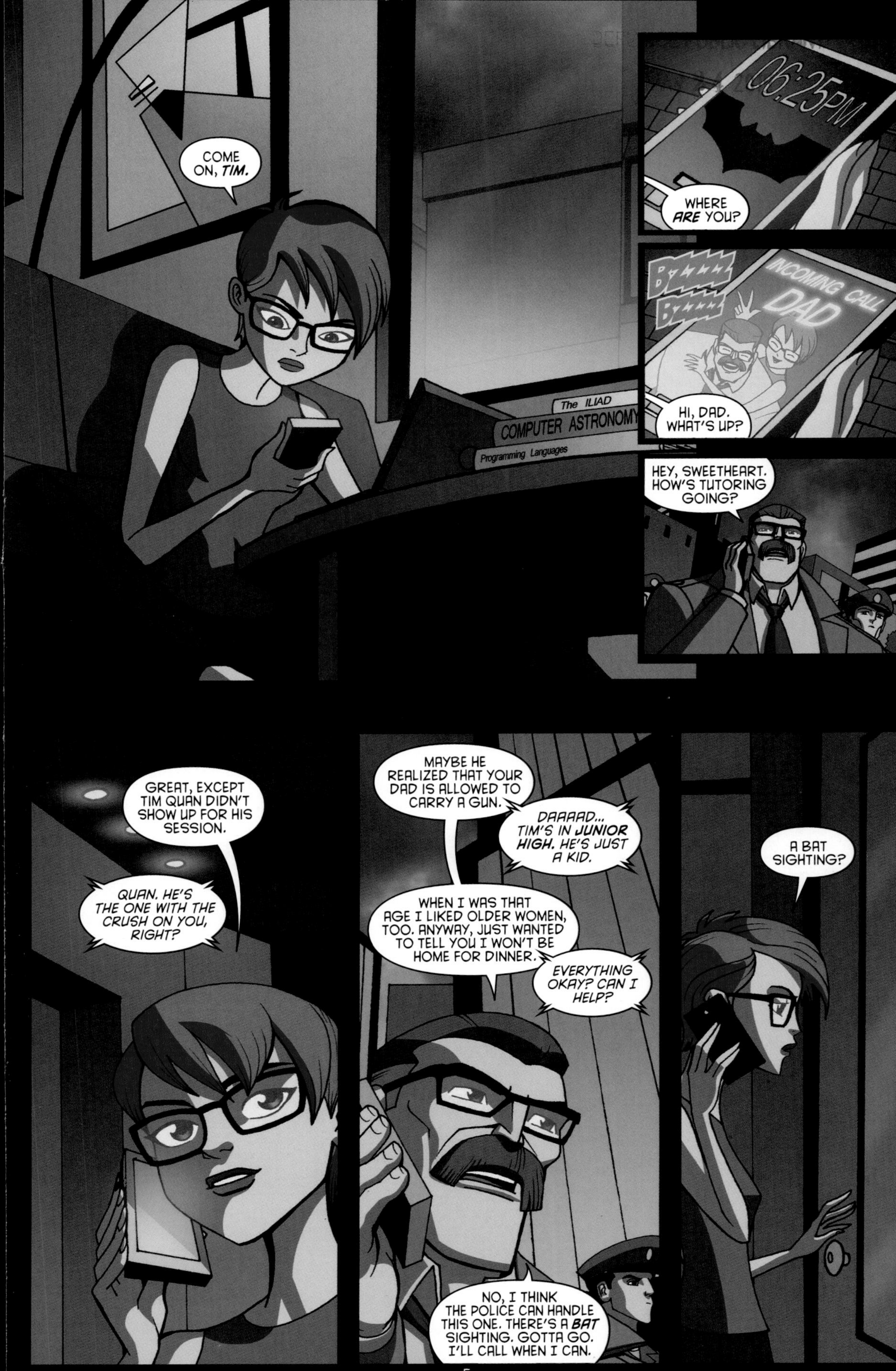
COME ON, TIM.
06:25PM
WHERE ARE YOU?
BZZZ BZZZ
INCOMING CALL DAD
HI, DAD. WHAT'S UP?
The ILIAD
COMPUTER ASTRONOMY
Programming Languages
HEY, SWEETHEART. HOW'S TUTORING GOING?
GREAT, EXCEPT TIM QUAN DIDN'T SHOW UP FOR HIS SESSION.
QUAN. HE'S THE ONE WITH THE CRUSH ON YOU, RIGHT?
MAYBE HE REALIZED THAT YOUR DAD IS ALLOWED TO CARRY A GUN.
DAAAAD... TIM'S IN JUNIOR HIGH. HE'S JUST A KID.
WHEN I WAS THAT AGE I LIKED OLDER WOMEN, TOO. ANYWAY, JUST WANTED TO TELL YOU I WON'T BE HOME FOR DINNER.
EVERYTHING OKAY? CAN I HELP?
NO, I THINK THE POLICE CAN HANDLE THIS ONE. THERE'S A BAT SIGHTING. GOTTA GO. I'LL CALL WHEN I CAN.
A BAT SIGHTING?

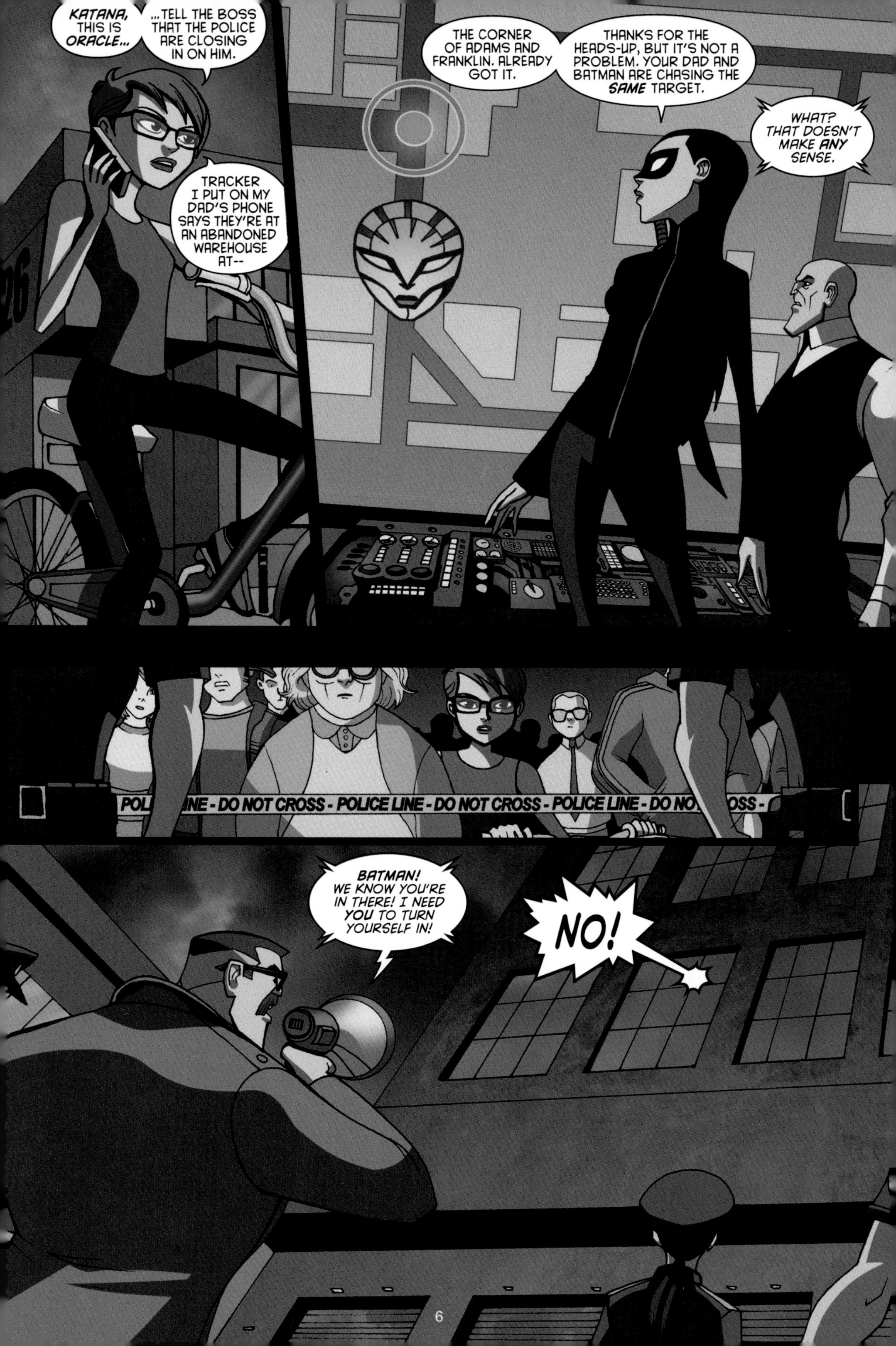
KATANA, THIS IS ORACLE...
...TELL THE BOSS THAT THE POLICE ARE CLOSING IN ON HIM.
TRACKER I PUT ON MY DAD'S PHONE SAYS THEY'RE AT AN ABANDONED WAREHOUSE AT--
THE CORNER OF ADAMS AND FRANKLIN. ALREADY GOT IT.
THANKS FOR THE HEADS-UP, BUT IT'S NOT A PROBLEM. YOUR DAD AND BATMAN ARE CHASING THE SAME TARGET.
WHAT? THAT DOESN'T MAKE ANY SENSE.
POLICE LINE - DO NOT CROSS - POLICE LINE - DO NOT CROSS - POLICE LINE - DO NO
BATMAN! WE KNOW YOU'RE IN THERE! I NEED YOU TO TURN YOURSELF IN!
NO!

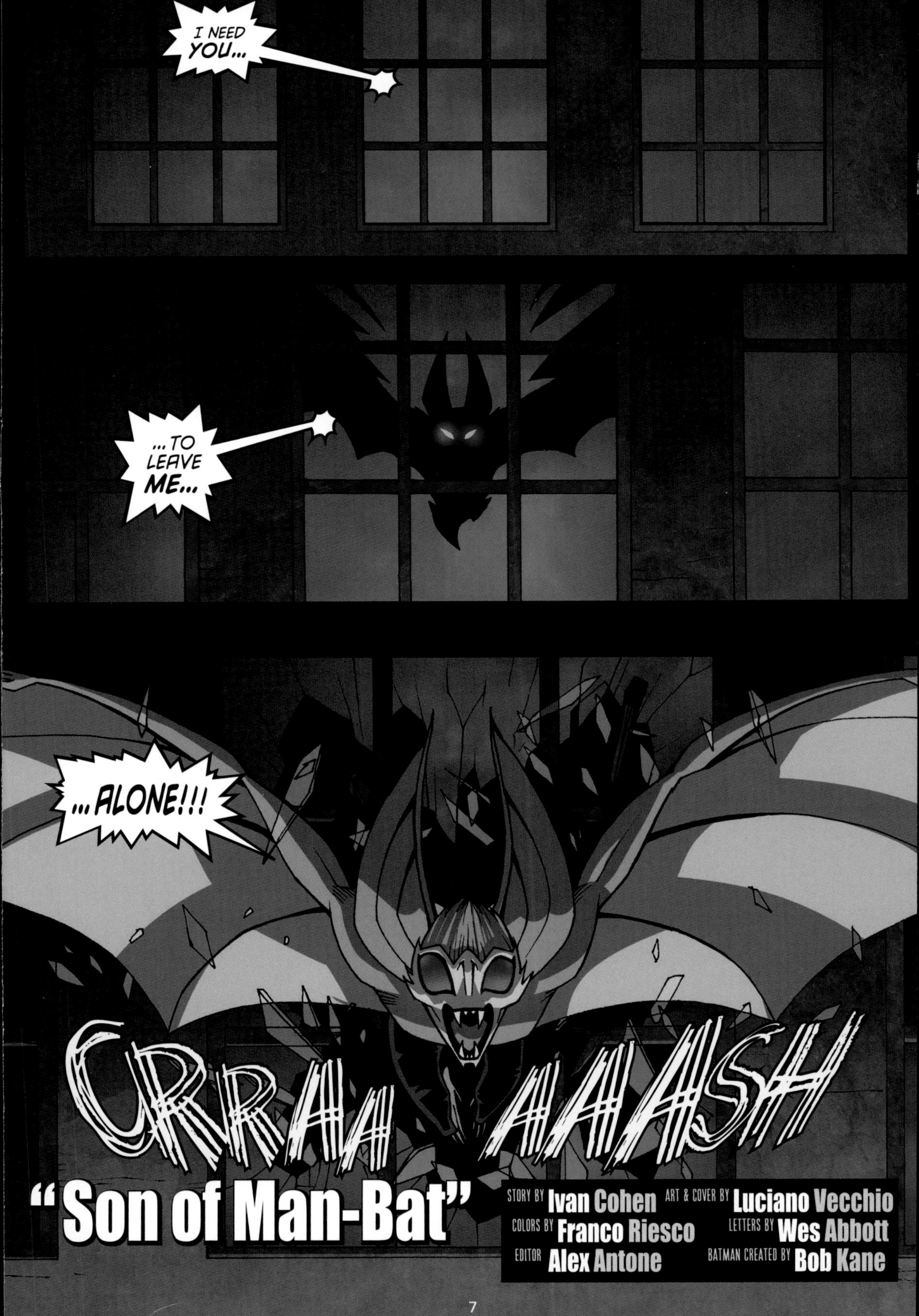
I NEED YOU...
...TO LEAVE ME...
...ALONE!!!
CRRAAAAASH
"Son of Man-Bat"
STORY BY Ivan Cohen
ART & COVER BY Luciano Vecchio
COLORS BY Franco Riesco
LETTERS BY Wes Abbott
EDITOR Alex Antone
BATMAN CREATED BY Bob Kane

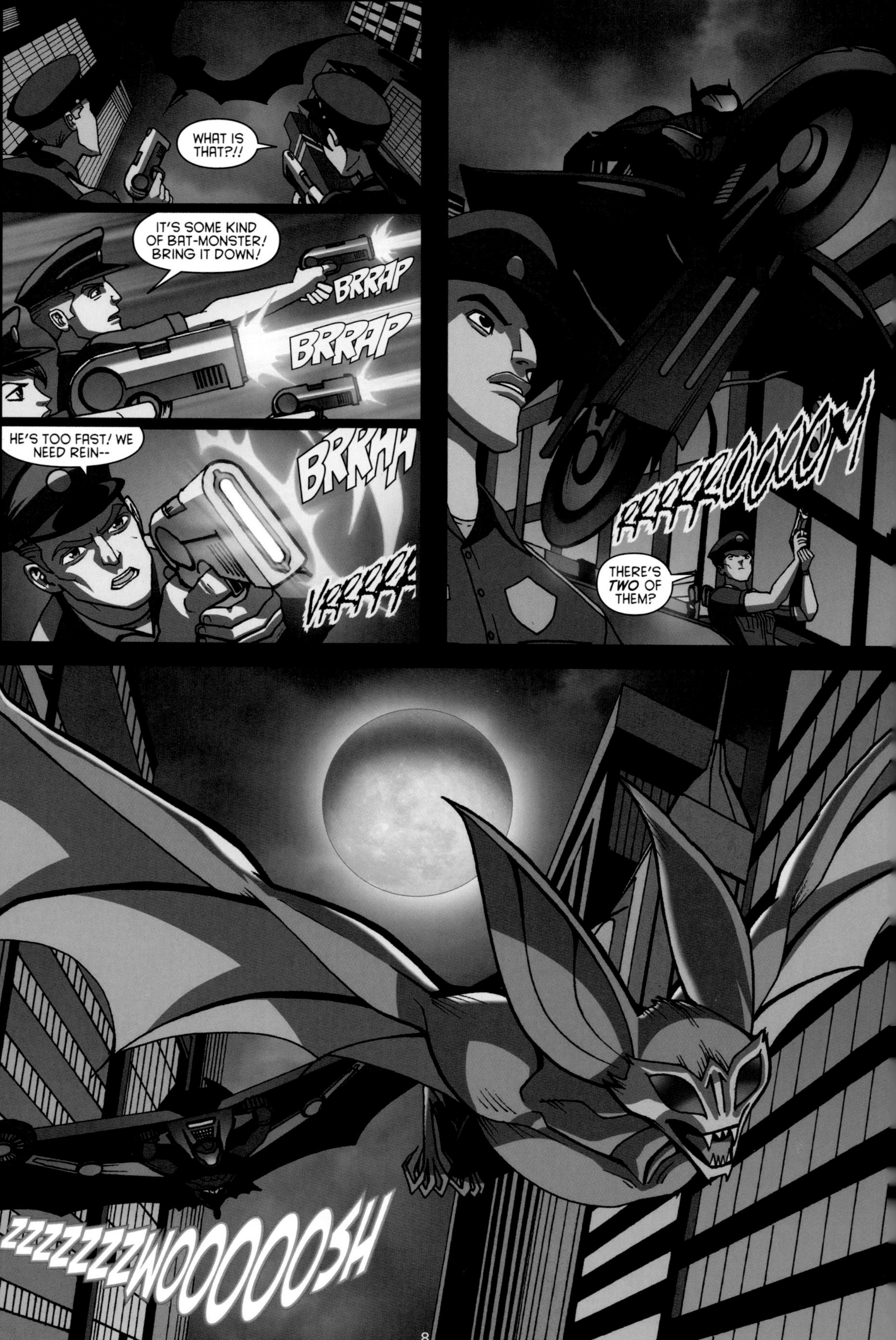
WHAT IS THAT?!!
IT'S SOME KIND OF BAT-MONSTER! BRING IT DOWN!
BRRAP
BRRAP
HE'S TOO FAST! WE NEED REIN--
BRRAAA
RRRRROOOOOM
THERE'S *TWO* OF THEM?
ZZZZZZZWOOOOOOSH

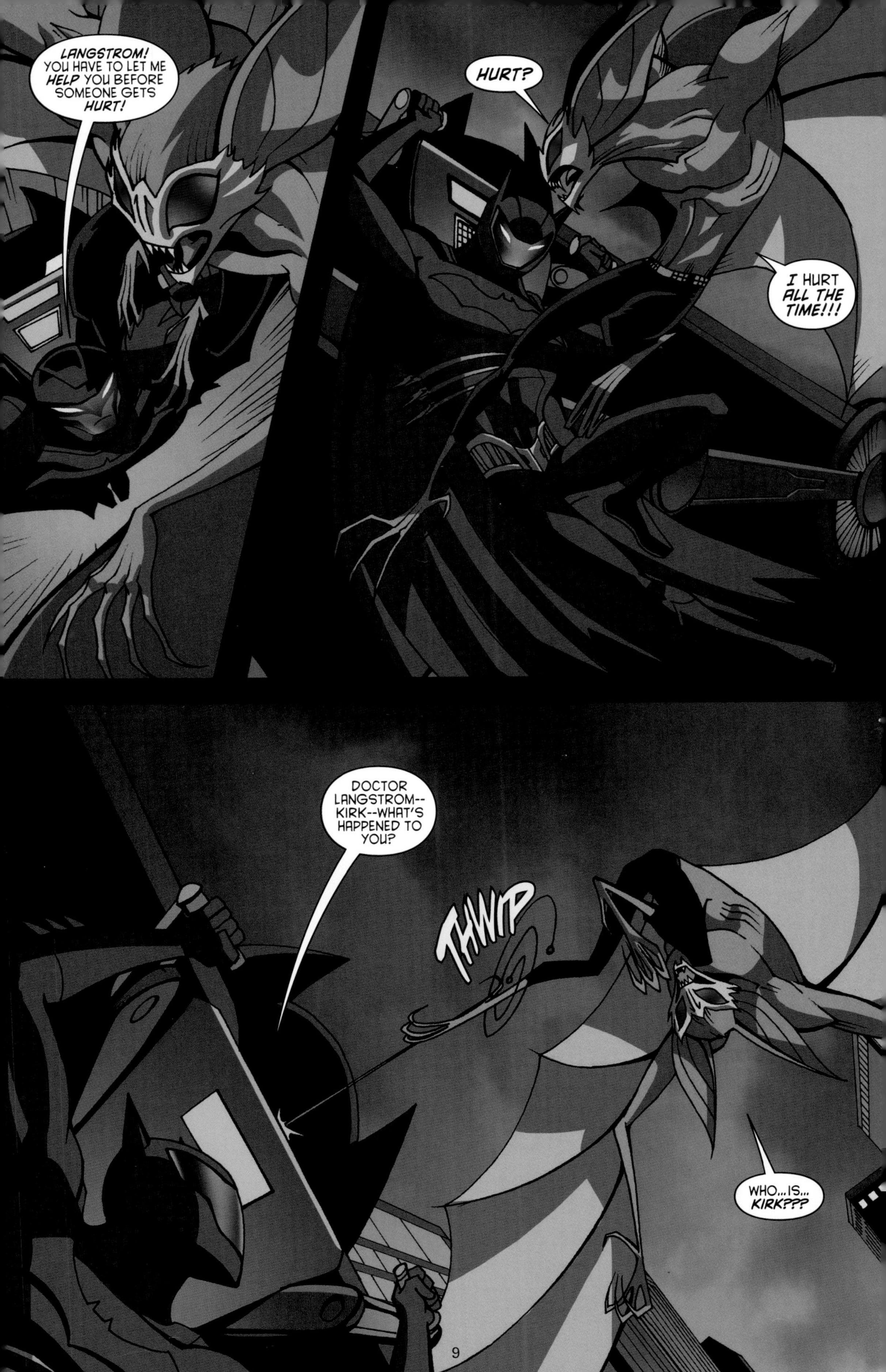
LANGSTROM! YOU HAVE TO LET ME HELP YOU BEFORE SOMEONE GETS HURT!
HURT?
I HURT ALL THE TIME!!!
DOCTOR LANGSTROM--KIRK--WHAT'S HAPPENED TO YOU?
THWIP
WHO...IS... KIRK???

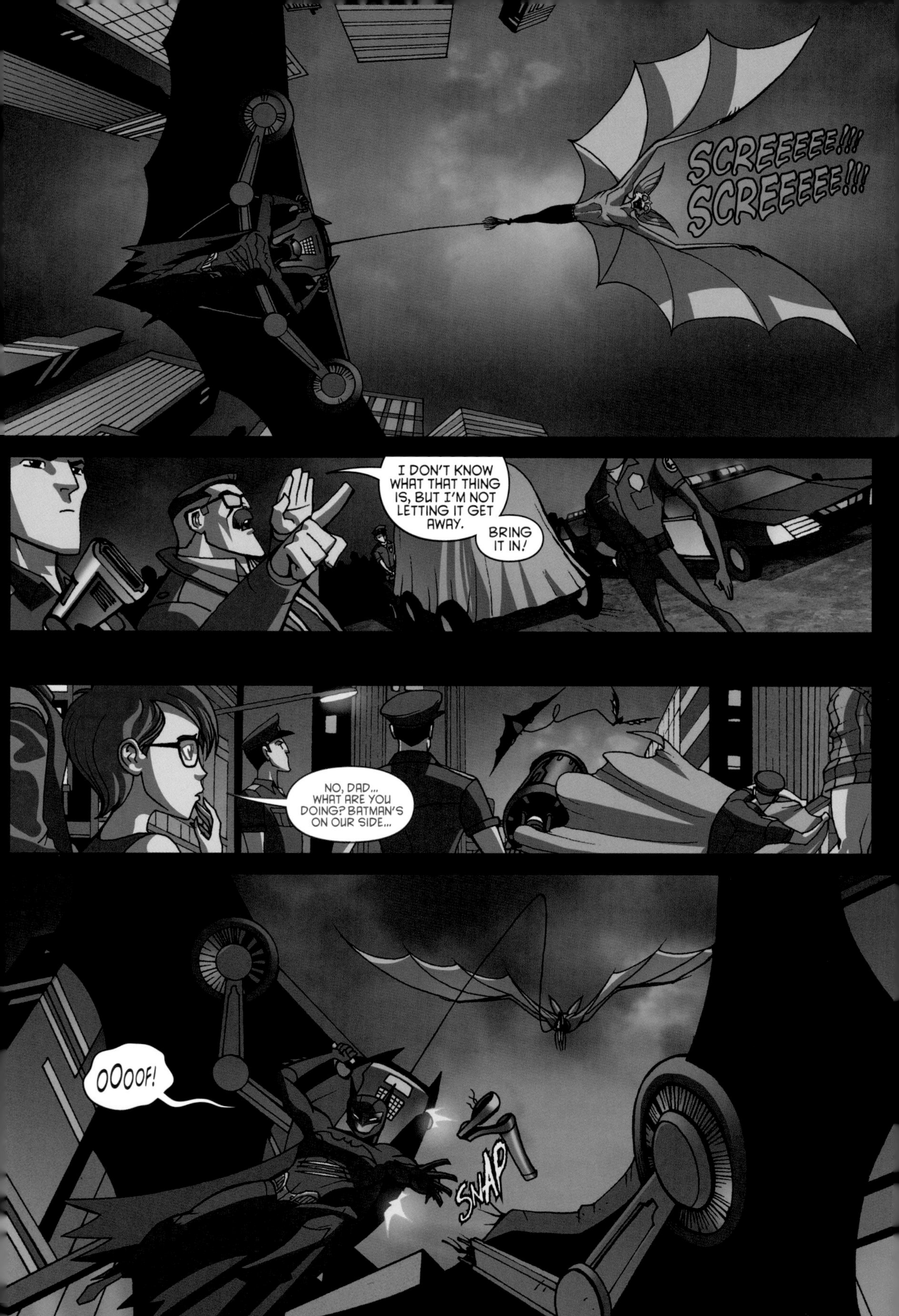
SCREEEEEE!!!
SCREEEEEE!!!
I DON'T KNOW WHAT THAT THING IS, BUT I'M NOT LETTING IT GET AWAY.
BRING IT IN!
NO, DAD... WHAT ARE YOU DOING? BATMAN'S ON OUR SIDE...
OOOOF!
SNAP

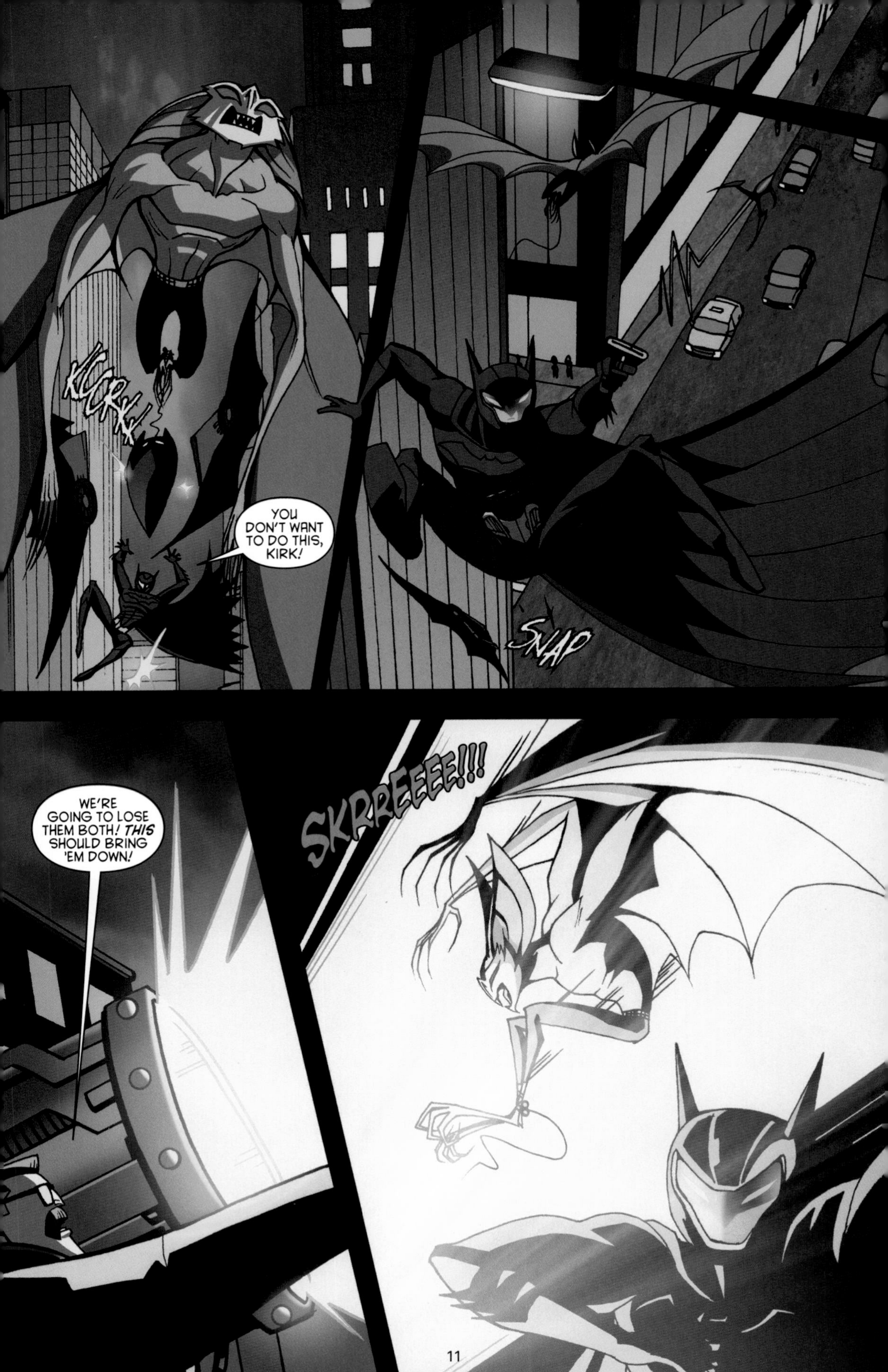
KKRKK!
YOU DON'T WANT TO DO THIS, KIRK!
SNAP
WE'RE GOING TO LOSE THEM BOTH! THIS SHOULD BRING 'EM DOWN!
SKRREEEEE!!!

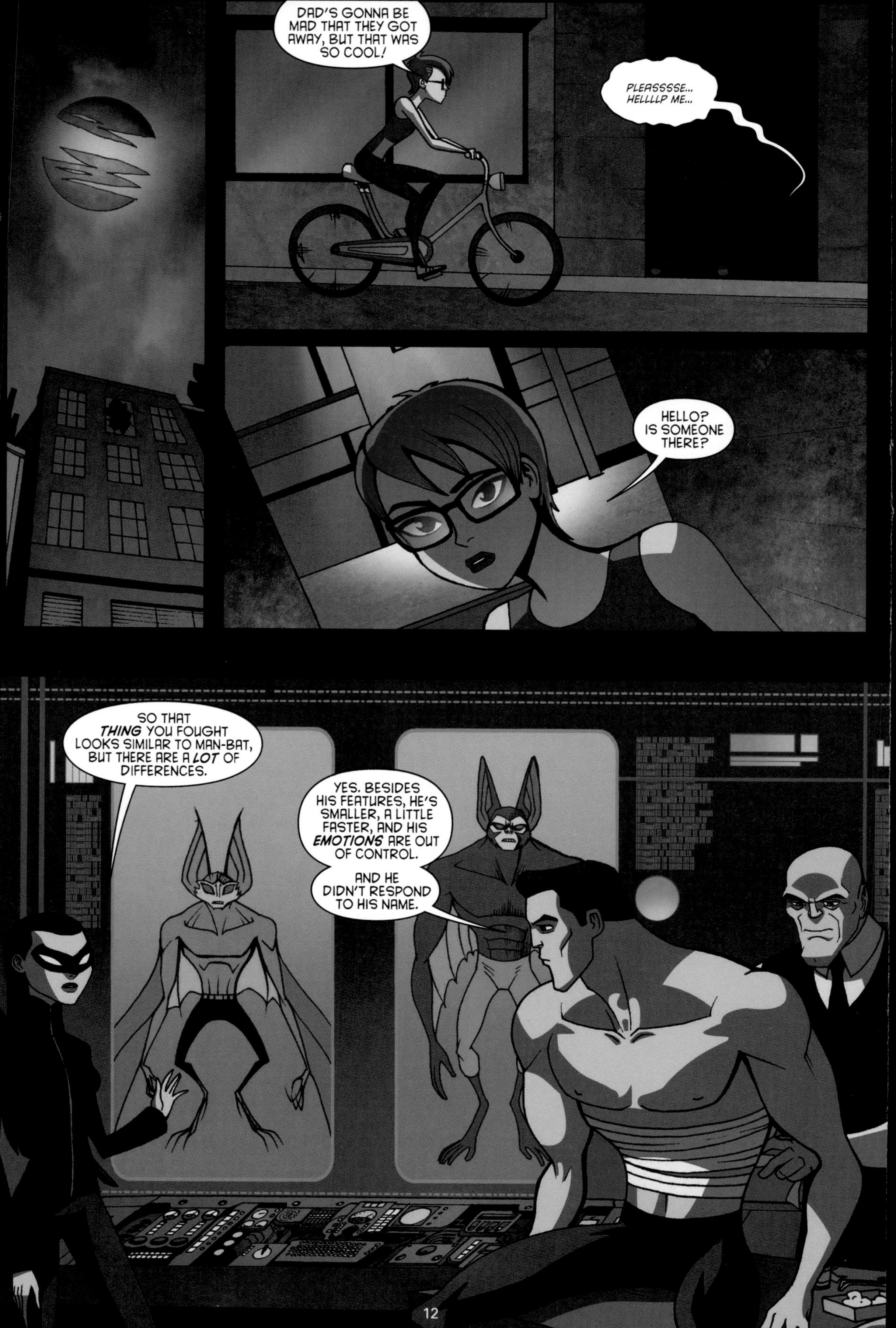
DAD'S GONNA BE MAD THAT THEY GOT AWAY, BUT THAT WAS SO COOL!
PLEASSSSE... HELLLLP ME...
HELLO? IS SOMEONE THERE?
SO THAT *THING* YOU FOUGHT LOOKS SIMILAR TO MAN-BAT, BUT THERE ARE A *LOT* OF DIFFERENCES.
YES. BESIDES HIS FEATURES, HE'S SMALLER, A LITTLE FASTER, AND HIS *EMOTIONS* ARE OUT OF CONTROL.
AND HE DIDN'T RESPOND TO HIS NAME.

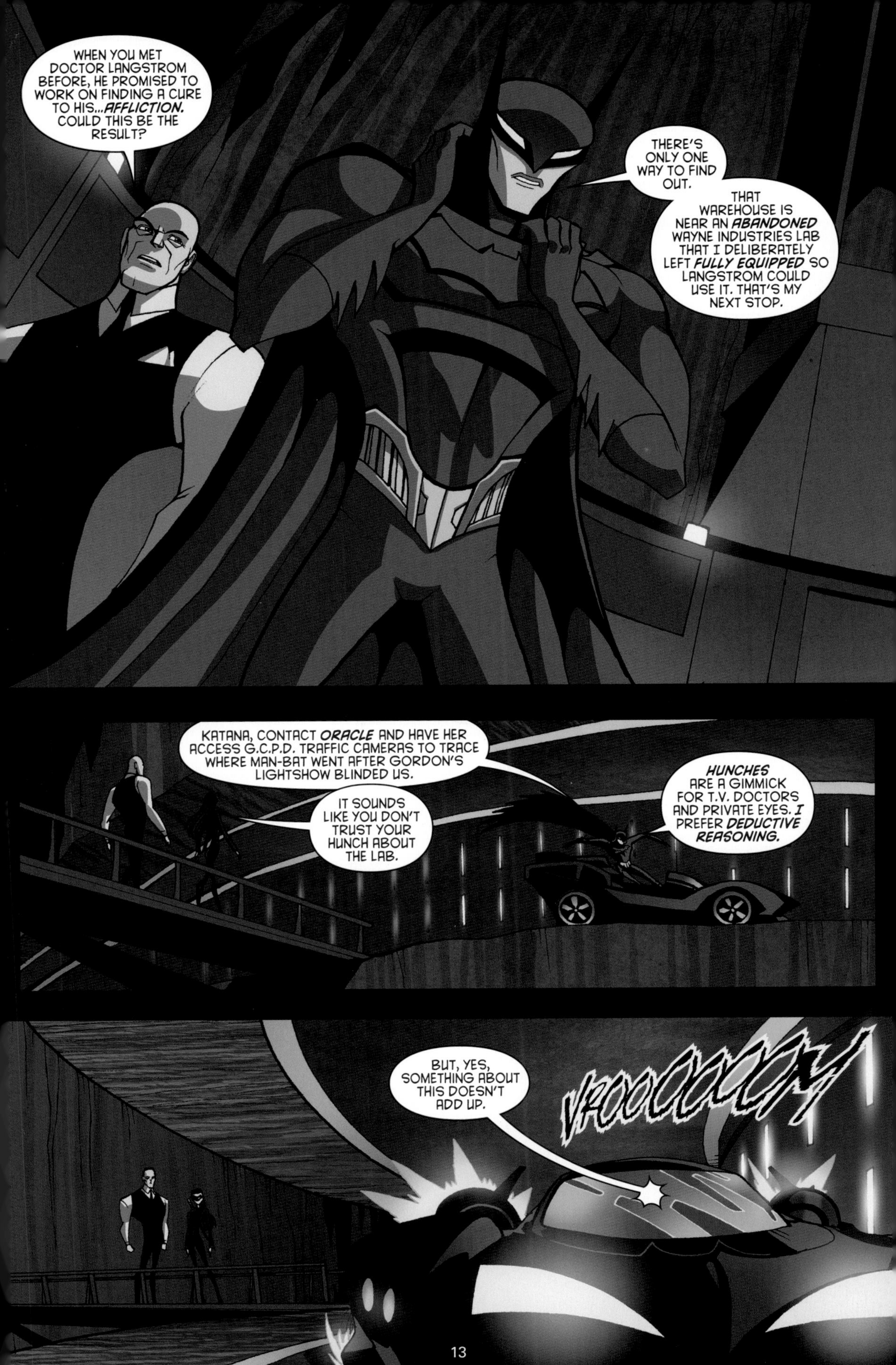
WHEN YOU MET DOCTOR LANGSTROM BEFORE, HE PROMISED TO WORK ON FINDING A CURE TO HIS...AFFLICTION. COULD THIS BE THE RESULT?
THERE'S ONLY ONE WAY TO FIND OUT.
THAT WAREHOUSE IS NEAR AN ABANDONED WAYNE INDUSTRIES LAB THAT I DELIBERATELY LEFT FULLY EQUIPPED SO LANGSTROM COULD USE IT. THAT'S MY NEXT STOP.
KATANA, CONTACT ORACLE AND HAVE HER ACCESS G.C.P.D. TRAFFIC CAMERAS TO TRACE WHERE MAN-BAT WENT AFTER GORDON'S LIGHTSHOW BLINDED US.
IT SOUNDS LIKE YOU DON'T TRUST YOUR HUNCH ABOUT THE LAB.
HUNCHES ARE A GIMMICK FOR T.V. DOCTORS AND PRIVATE EYES. I PREFER DEDUCTIVE REASONING.
BUT, YES, SOMETHING ABOUT THIS DOESN'T ADD UP.
VROOOOOOOM

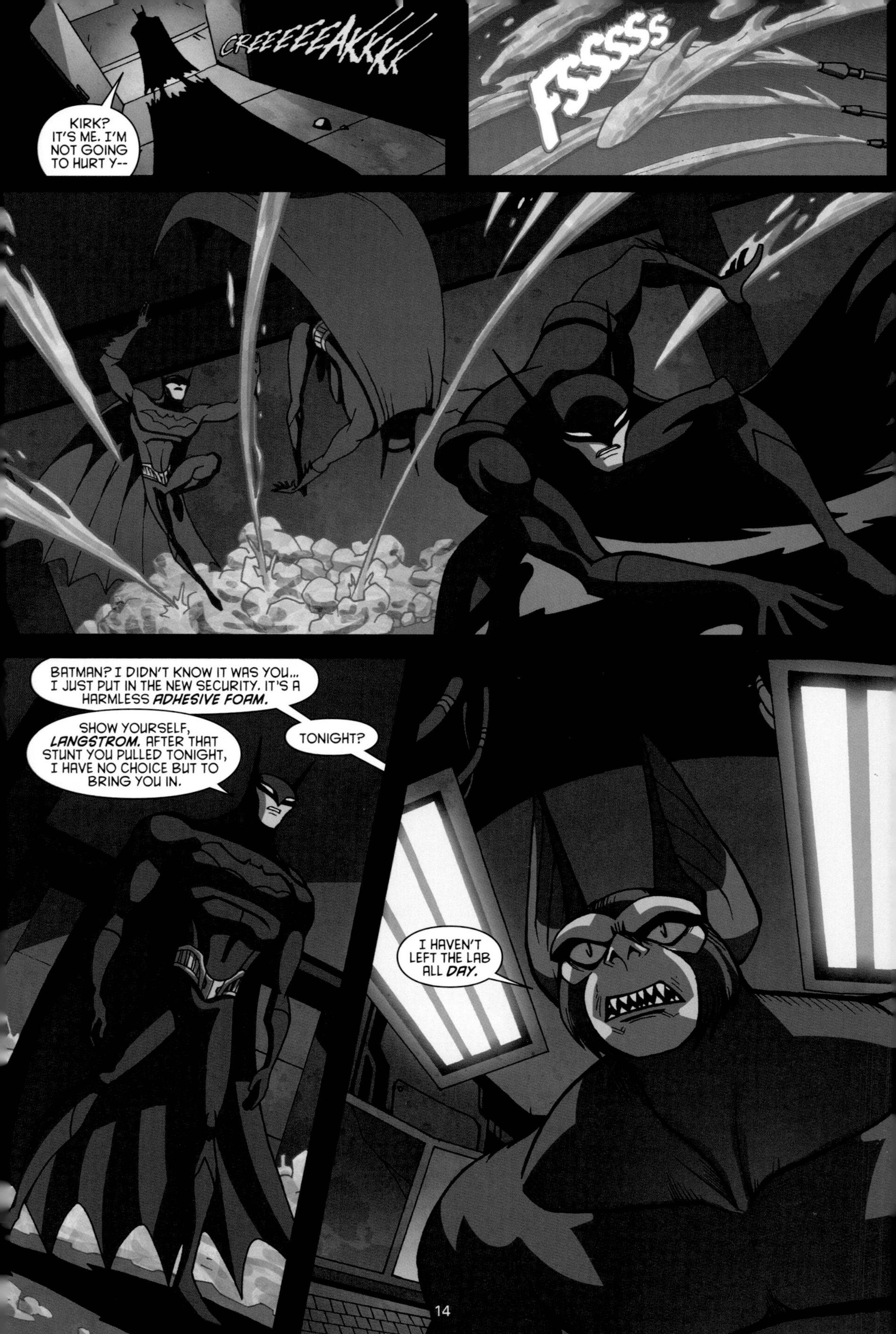
CREEEEEEAKKKK
KIRK? IT'S ME. I'M NOT GOING TO HURT Y--
FSSSSS
BATMAN? I DIDN'T KNOW IT WAS YOU... I JUST PUT IN THE NEW SECURITY. IT'S A HARMLESS ADHESIVE FOAM.
SHOW YOURSELF, LANGSTROM. AFTER THAT STUNT YOU PULLED TONIGHT, I HAVE NO CHOICE BUT TO BRING YOU IN.
TONIGHT?
I HAVEN'T LEFT THE LAB ALL DAY.

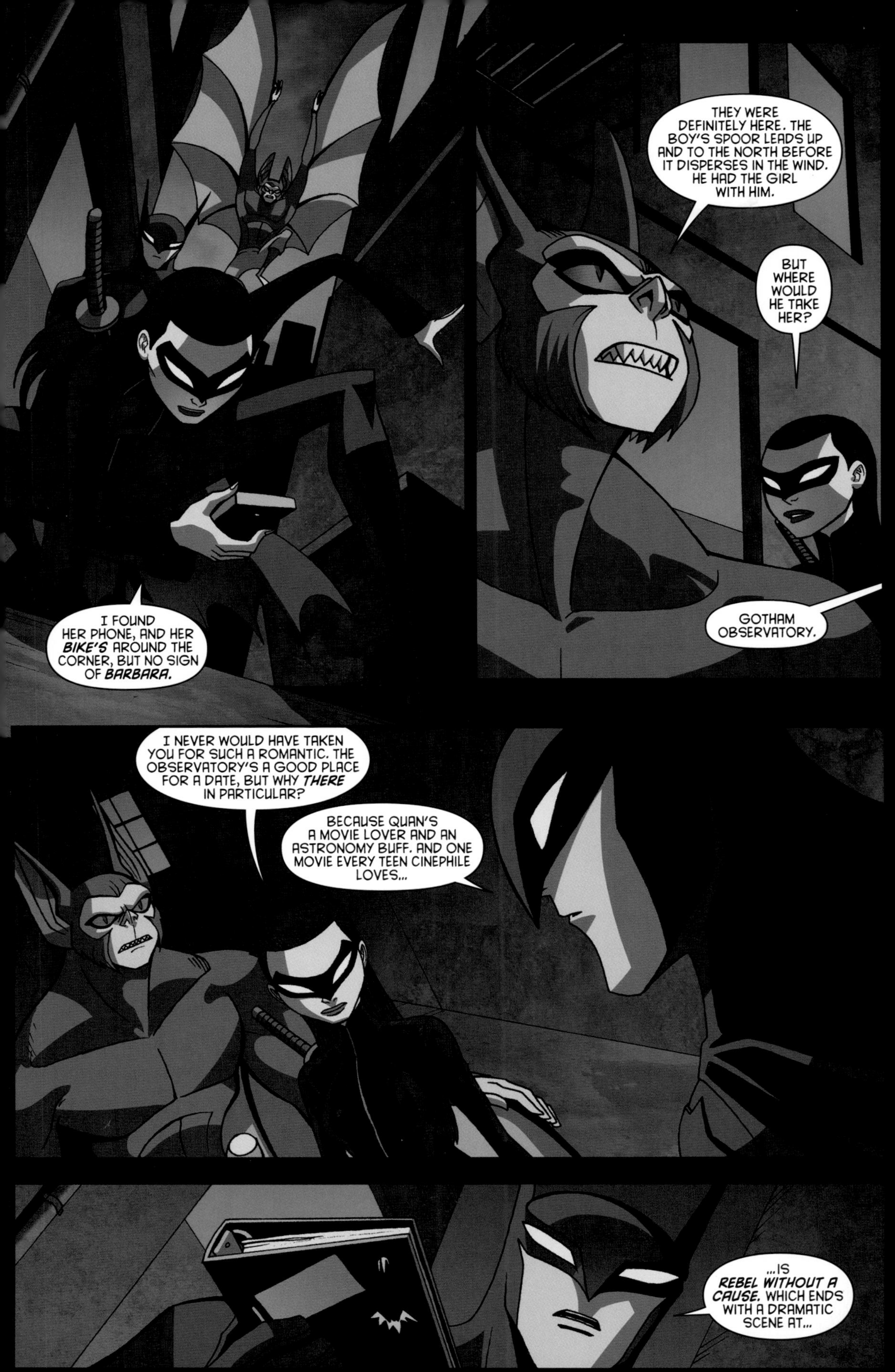
I FOUND HER PHONE, AND HER *BIKE'S* AROUND THE CORNER, BUT NO SIGN OF *BARBARA.*
THEY WERE DEFINITELY HERE. THE BOY'S SPOOR LEADS UP AND TO THE NORTH BEFORE IT DISPERSES IN THE WIND. HE HAD THE GIRL WITH HIM.
BUT WHERE WOULD HE TAKE HER?
GOTHAM OBSERVATORY.
I NEVER WOULD HAVE TAKEN YOU FOR SUCH A ROMANTIC. THE OBSERVATORY'S A GOOD PLACE FOR A DATE, BUT WHY *THERE* IN PARTICULAR?
BECAUSE QUAN'S A MOVIE LOVER AND AN ASTRONOMY BUFF. AND ONE MOVIE EVERY TEEN CINEPHILE LOVES...
...IS *REBEL WITHOUT A CAUSE.* WHICH ENDS WITH A DRAMATIC SCENE AT...

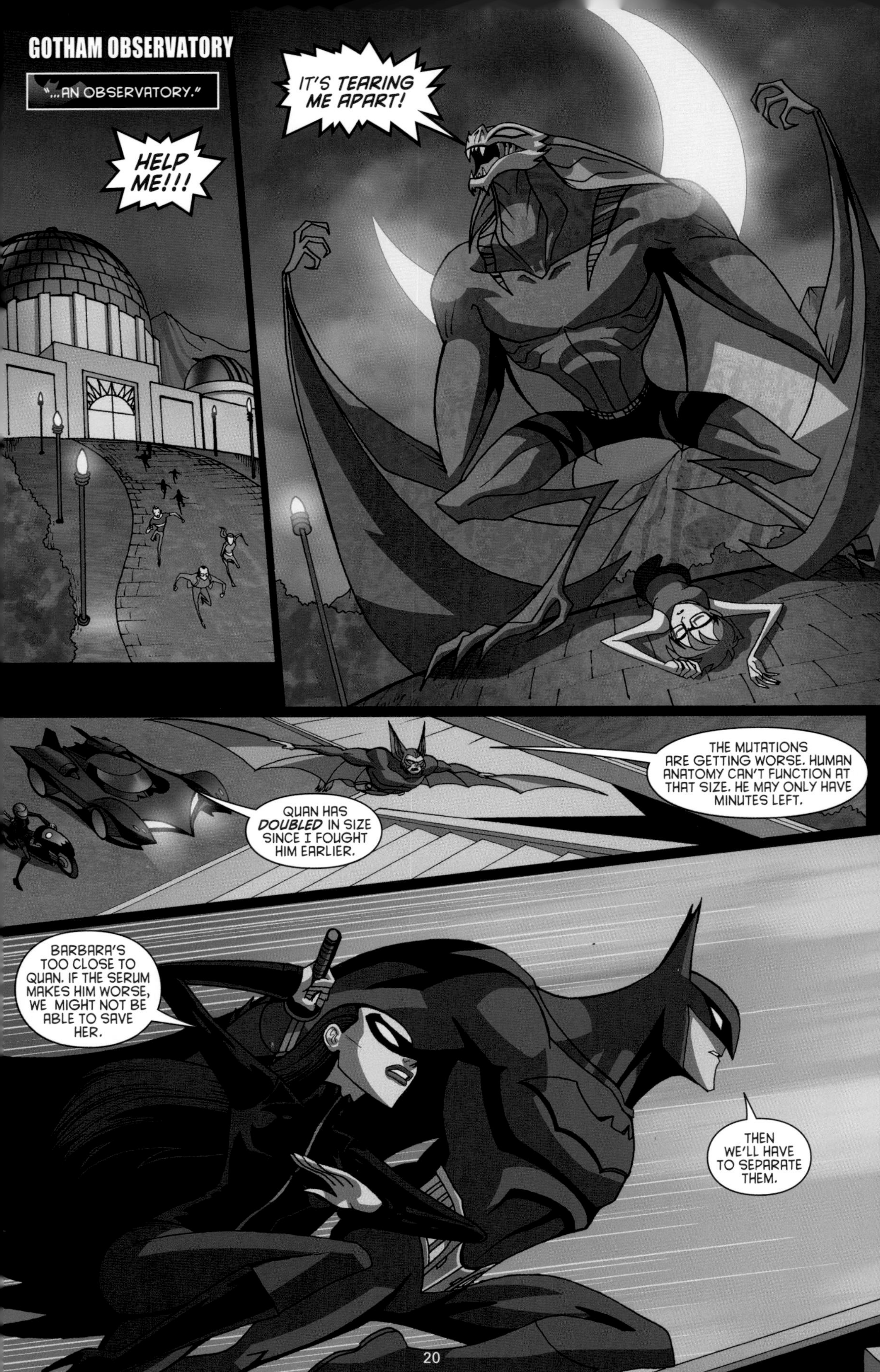
GOTHAM OBSERVATORY
"...AN OBSERVATORY."
HELP ME!!!
IT'S TEARING ME APART!
QUAN HAS DOUBLED IN SIZE SINCE I FOUGHT HIM EARLIER.
THE MUTATIONS ARE GETTING WORSE. HUMAN ANATOMY CAN'T FUNCTION AT THAT SIZE. HE MAY ONLY HAVE MINUTES LEFT.
BARBARA'S TOO CLOSE TO QUAN. IF THE SERUM MAKES HIM WORSE, WE MIGHT NOT BE ABLE TO SAVE HER.
THEN WE'LL HAVE TO SEPARATE THEM.

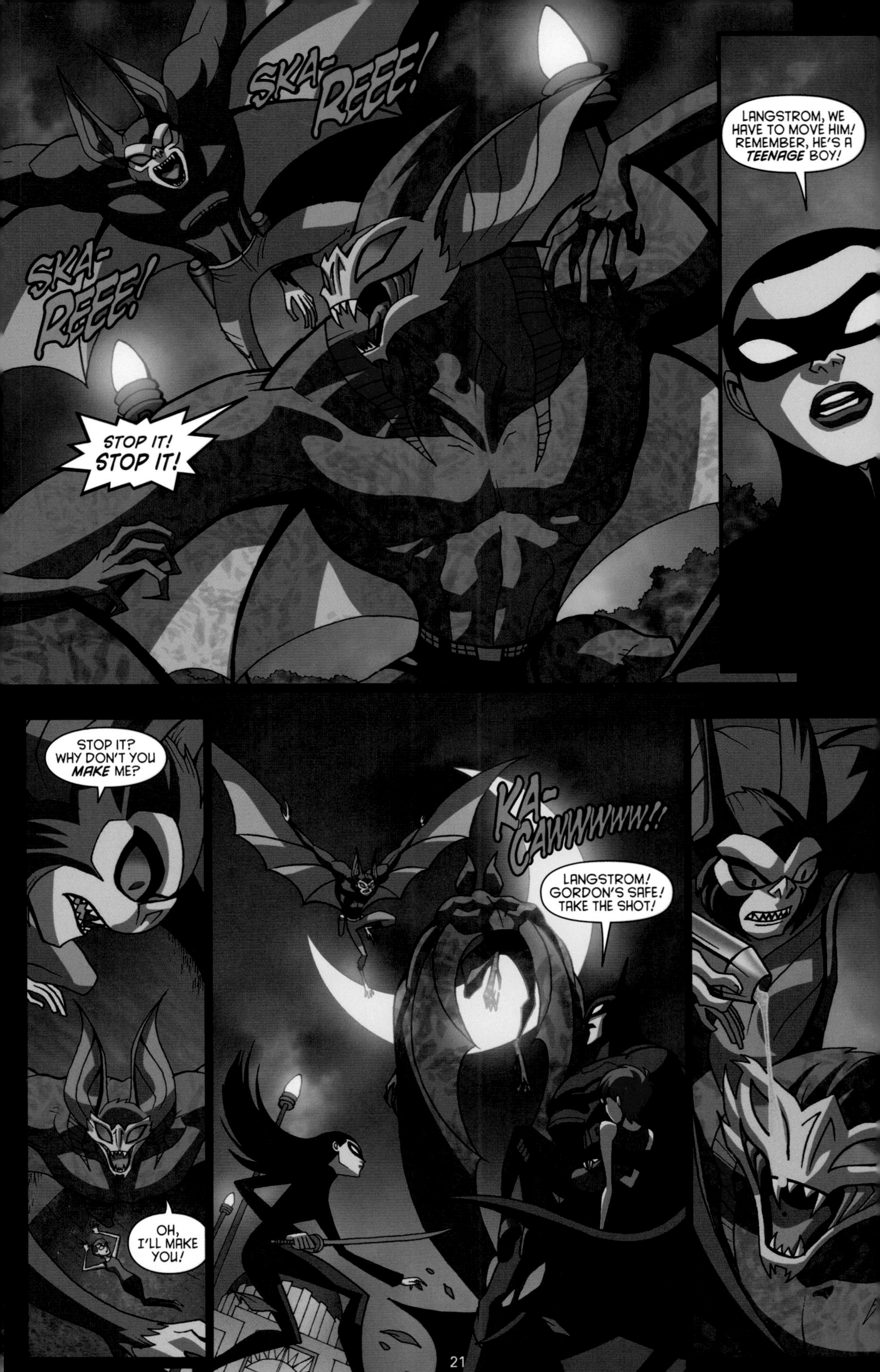

SKA-REEE!
SKA-REEE!
STOP IT! STOP IT!
LANGSTROM, WE HAVE TO MOVE HIM! REMEMBER, HE'S A *TEENAGE* BOY!
STOP IT? WHY DON'T YOU *MAKE* ME?
OH, I'LL MAKE YOU!
KA-CAWWWWW!!
LANGSTROM! GORDON'S SAFE! TAKE THE SHOT!

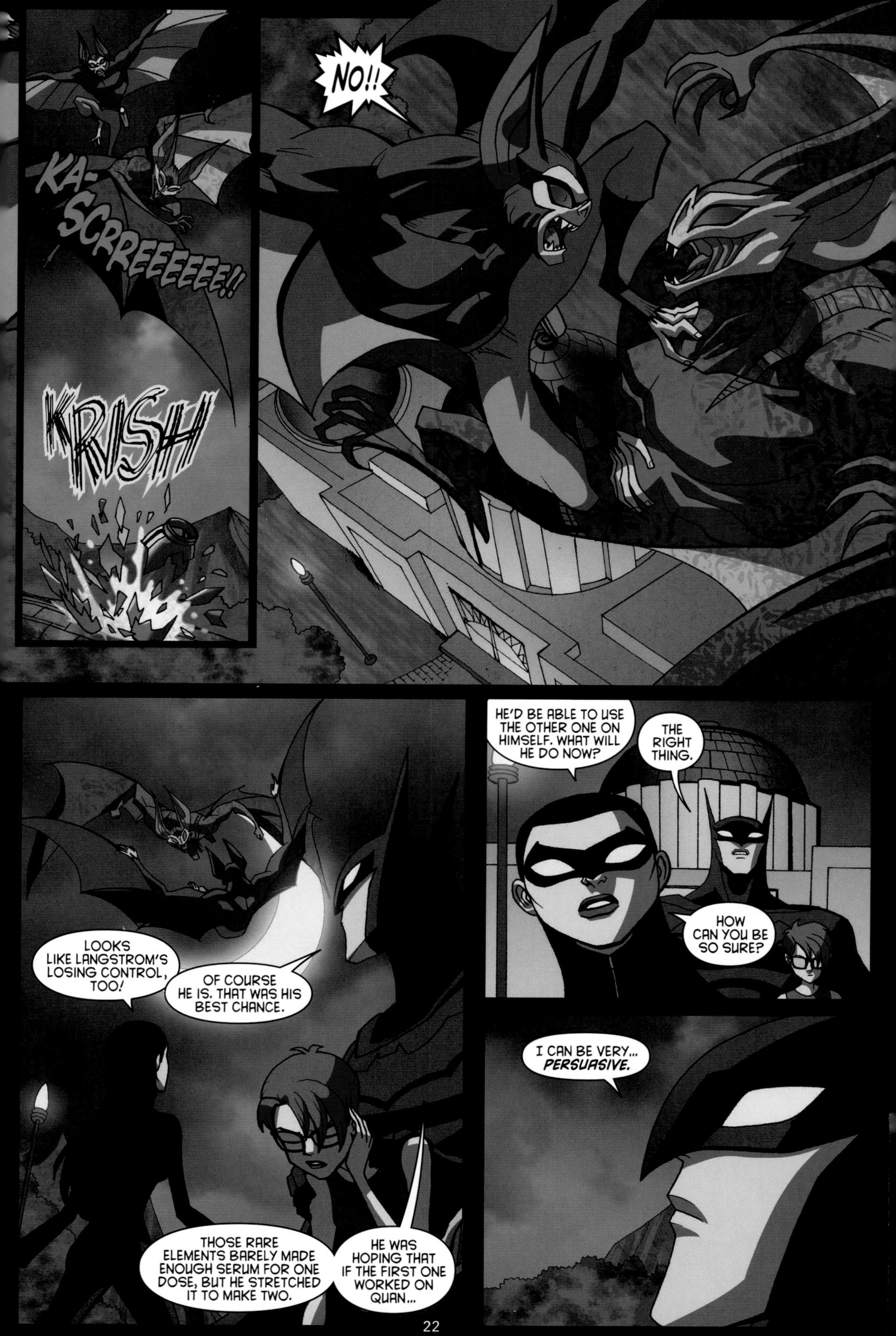
KA-SCRREEEEEEE!!
KRISH
NO!!
LOOKS LIKE LANGSTROM'S LOSING CONTROL, TOO!
OF COURSE HE IS. THAT WAS HIS BEST CHANCE.
THOSE RARE ELEMENTS BARELY MADE ENOUGH SERUM FOR ONE DOSE, BUT HE STRETCHED IT TO MAKE TWO.
HE WAS HOPING THAT IF THE FIRST ONE WORKED ON QUAN...
HE'D BE ABLE TO USE THE OTHER ONE ON HIMSELF. WHAT WILL HE DO NOW?
THE RIGHT THING.
HOW CAN YOU BE SO SURE?
I CAN BE VERY... PERSUASIVE.

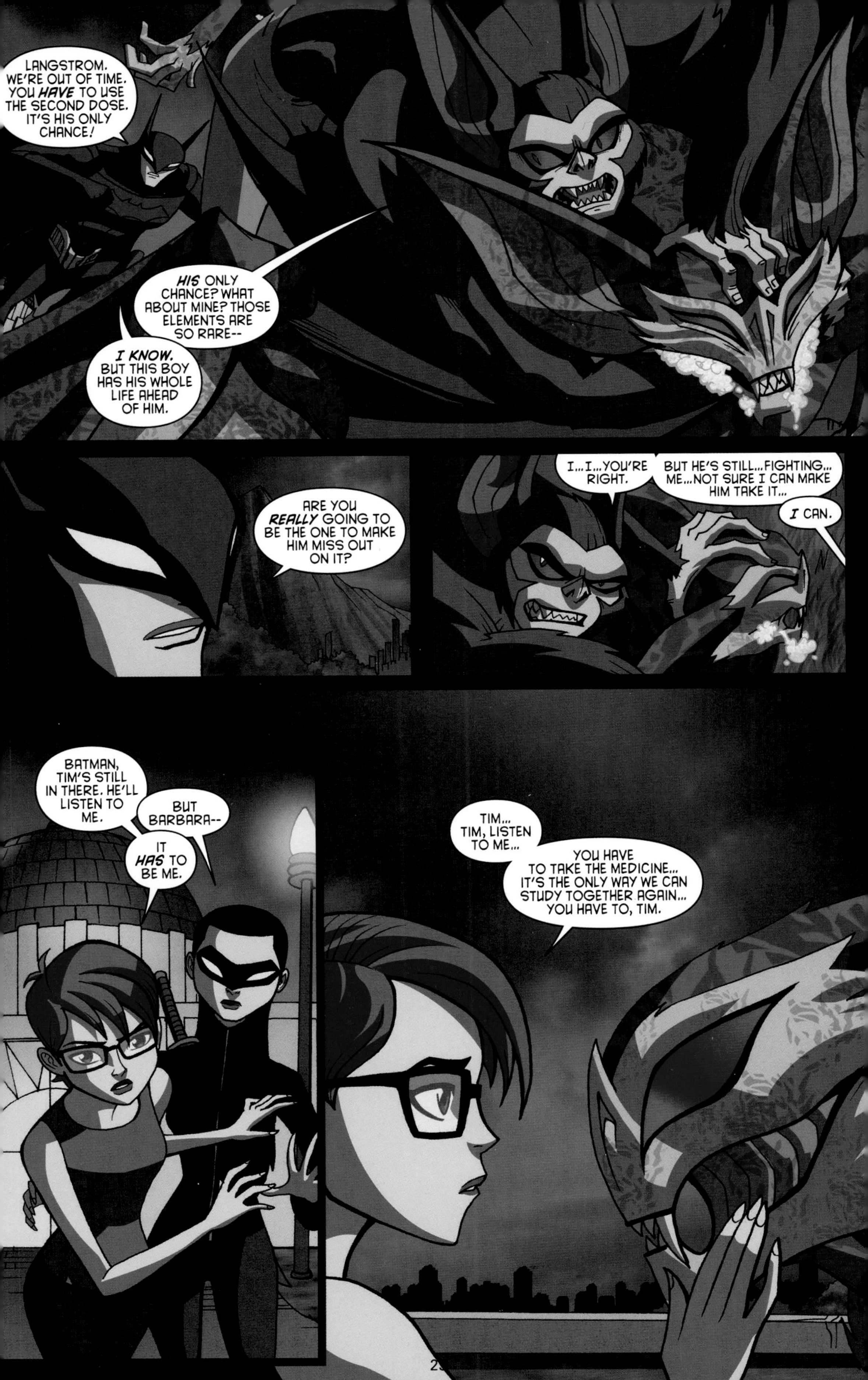

LANGSTROM. WE'RE OUT OF TIME. YOU *HAVE* TO USE THE SECOND DOSE. IT'S HIS ONLY CHANCE!
HIS ONLY CHANCE? WHAT ABOUT MINE? THOSE ELEMENTS ARE SO RARE--
I KNOW. BUT THIS BOY HAS HIS WHOLE LIFE AHEAD OF HIM.
ARE YOU *REALLY* GOING TO BE THE ONE TO MAKE HIM MISS OUT ON IT?
I...I...YOU'RE RIGHT.
BUT HE'S STILL...FIGHTING... ME...NOT SURE I CAN MAKE HIM TAKE IT...
I CAN.
BATMAN, TIM'S STILL IN THERE. HE'LL LISTEN TO ME.
BUT BARBARA--
IT *HAS* TO BE ME.
TIM... TIM, LISTEN TO ME...
YOU HAVE TO TAKE THE MEDICINE... IT'S THE ONLY WAY WE CAN STUDY TOGETHER AGAIN... YOU HAVE TO, TIM.

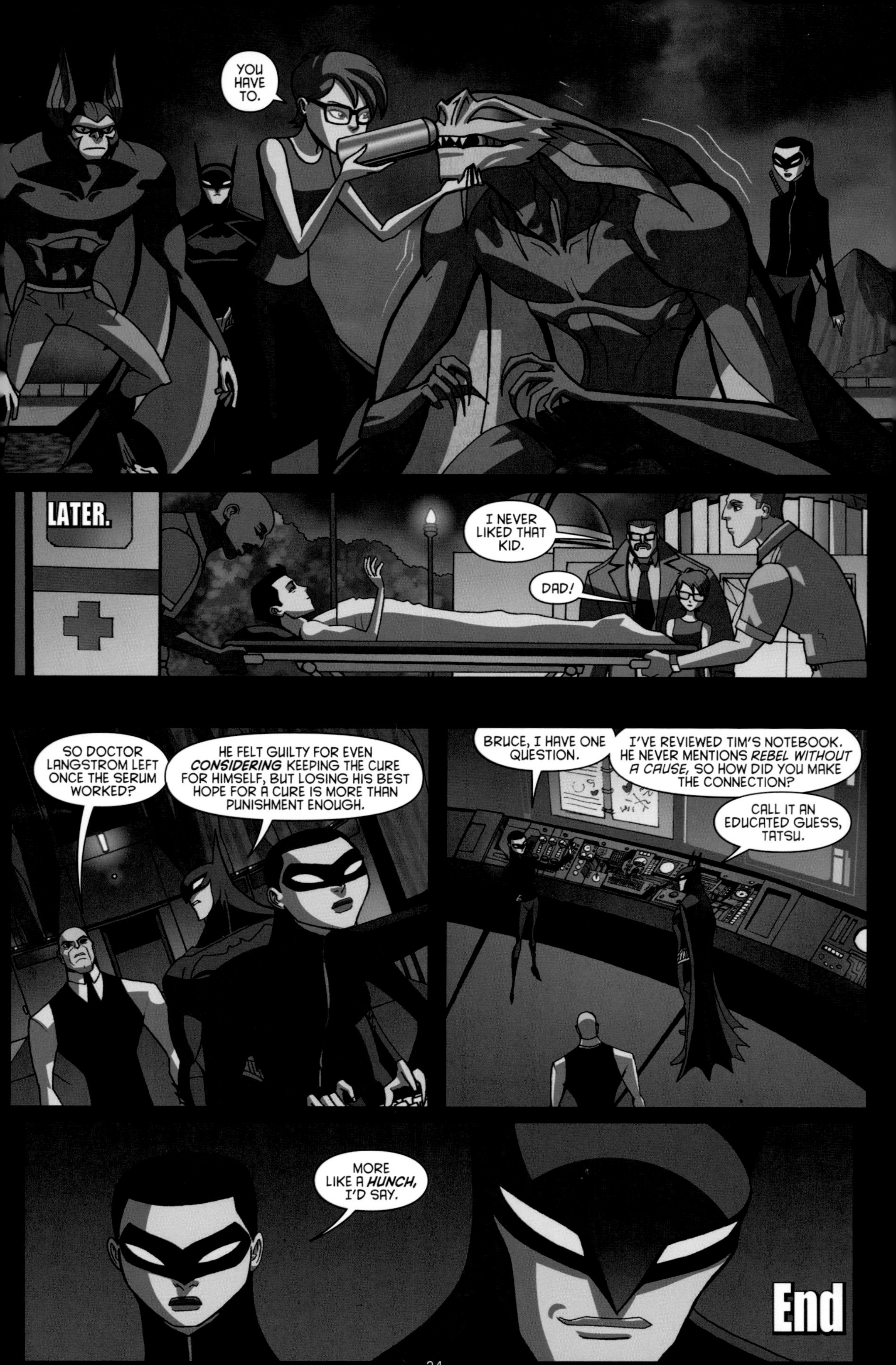
YOU HAVE TO.
LATER.
I NEVER LIKED THAT KID.
DAD!
SO DOCTOR LANGSTROM LEFT ONCE THE SERUM WORKED?
HE FELT GUILTY FOR EVEN CONSIDERING KEEPING THE CURE FOR HIMSELF, BUT LOSING HIS BEST HOPE FOR A CURE IS MORE THAN PUNISHMENT ENOUGH.
BRUCE, I HAVE ONE QUESTION.
I'VE REVIEWED TIM'S NOTEBOOK. HE NEVER MENTIONS REBEL WITHOUT A CAUSE, SO HOW DID YOU MAKE THE CONNECTION?
CALL IT AN EDUCATED GUESS, TATSU.
MORE LIKE A HUNCH, I'D SAY.
End

CREATORS

IVAN COHEN — WRITER

A former editor and media-development executive at DC Comics, Ivan Cohen worked on the DC Universe line of direct-to-video animated movies as well as the popular TV series *Smallville*, *Batman: The Brave and the Bold*, and *Young Justice*. As a writer, Cohen's recent credits include the *Green Lantern: The Animated Series* comic book, articles for *Time Out* magazine, and an episode of the upcoming Cartoon Network television series *Beware The Batman*. The co-producer of *Secret Origin: The Story of DC Comics* [2010], he is a consultant on the upcoming PBS documentary *Superheroes: The Never-Ending Battle*.

LUCIANO VECCHIO — ILLUSTRATOR

Luciano Vecchio currently lives in Buenos Aires, Argentina. With experience in illustration, animation, and comics, his works have been published in the US, Spain, the UK, France, and Argentina. His credits include Ben 10 [DC Comics], Cruel Thing [Norma], Unseen Tribe [Zuda Comics], Sentinels [Drumfish Productions], and several DC Super Heroes books for Stone Arch Books.

GLOSSARY

adhesive [ad·HEE·siv]--designed to stick to something

affliction [uh·FLIKT·shuhn]--something, like as a disease, that causes pain or suffering

antidote [AN·ti·doht]--a substance that stops the harmful effects of a poison

cinephile [SIN·i·fahyl]--a devoted moviegoer, especially one knowledgeable about cinema (or the movie business)

deductive [di·DUHK·tiv]--using logic or reason to form a conclusion or opinion about something

deliberately [di·LIB·er·uht·lee]--in a way that is meant, intended, or planned

gimmick [GIM·ick]--a method or trick

mutations [myoo·TAY·shuhns]--changes in the genes of a plant or animal that cause physical characteristics that are different from what is normal

oracle [OR·uh·kuhl]--a person who has a lot of knowledge about something and whose opinions and advice are highly valued.

spoor [SPOOR]--a track or trail, especially that of a wild animal pursued as game.

VISUAL QUESTIONS & PROMPTS

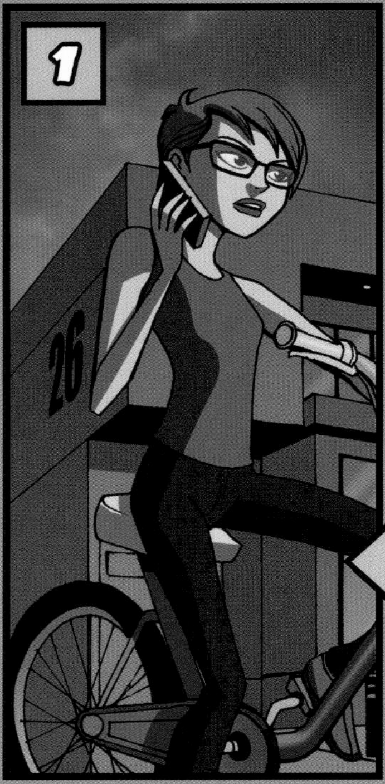
1
26

1. Barbara Gordon's secret identity is Oracle. Read the definition of "oracle" in the glossary. Based on that definition, why do you think she chose the nickname Oracle? What skills does she have that explain it?

2. Why is Barbara Gordon's speech bubble lighter in color here? Why did the book's creators decide to do this?

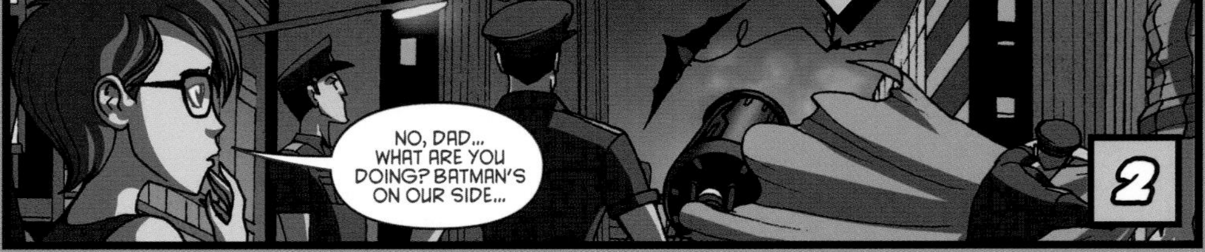
NO, DAD... WHAT ARE YOU DOING? BATMAN'S ON OUR SIDE...
2

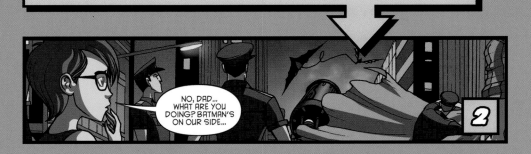

3. Whose voice does Barbara hear from the alleyway? Find two clues to the person's identity.

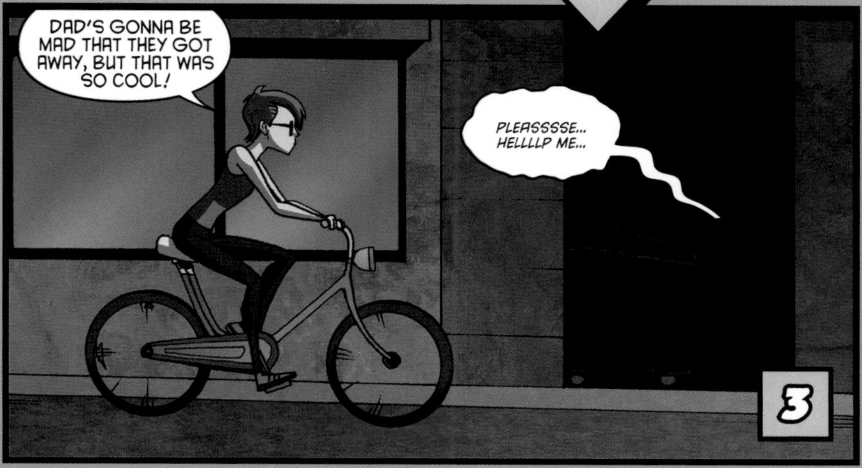
DAD'S GONNA BE MAD THAT THEY GOT AWAY, BUT THAT WAS SO COOL!
PLEASSSSE... HELLLLP ME...
3

4. Batman has lots of tools and gadgets. Of all the tools he uses in this book, which one would you want to have the most? Why?

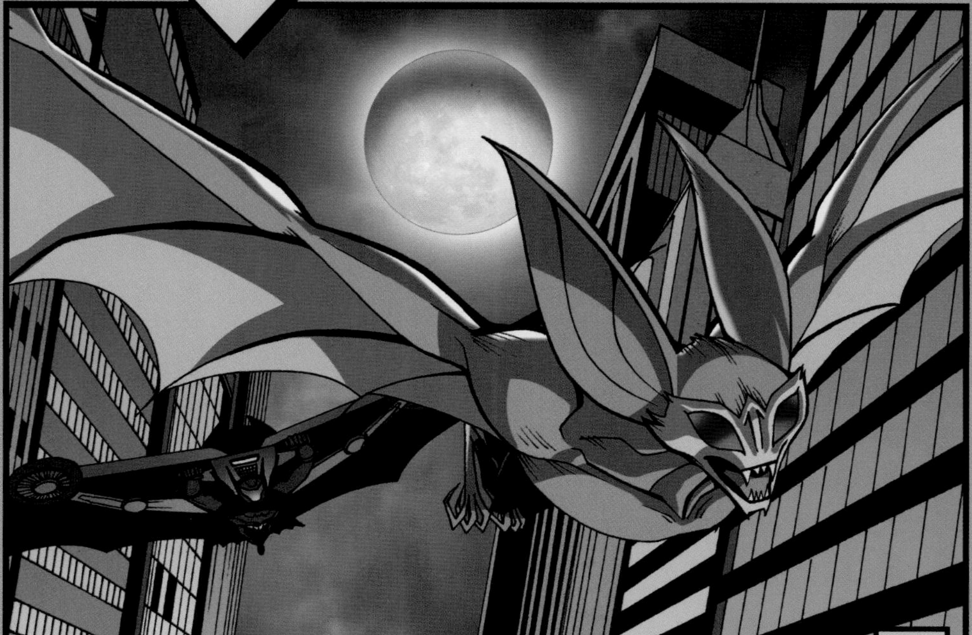
4

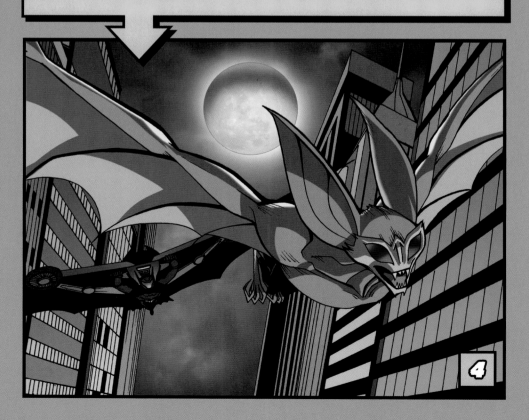

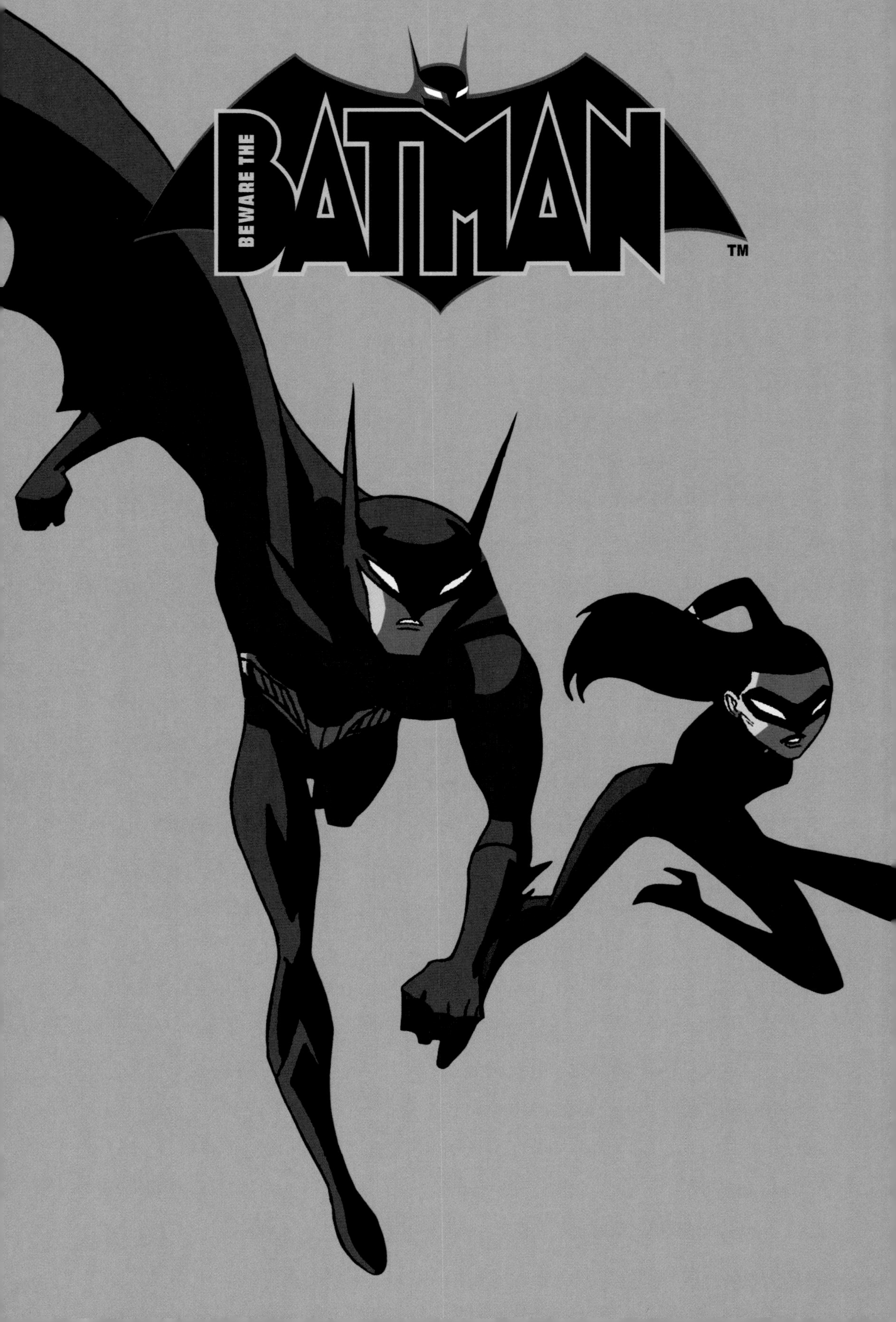
BEWARE THE
BATMAN
TM

READ THEM ALL!

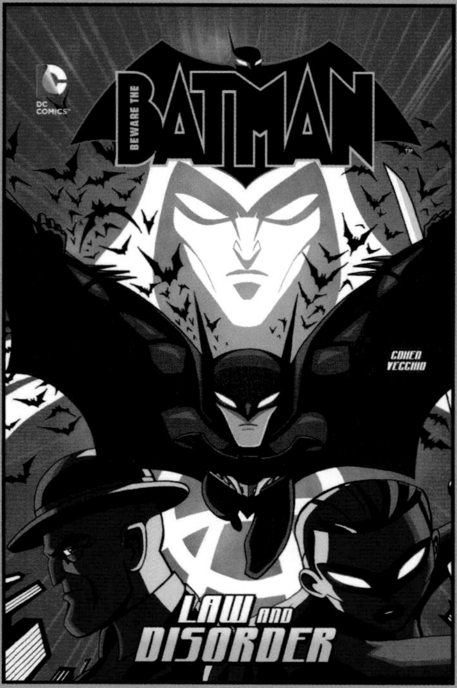
DC COMICS
BEWARE THE BATMAN
COHEN
VECCHIO
LAW AND DISORDER

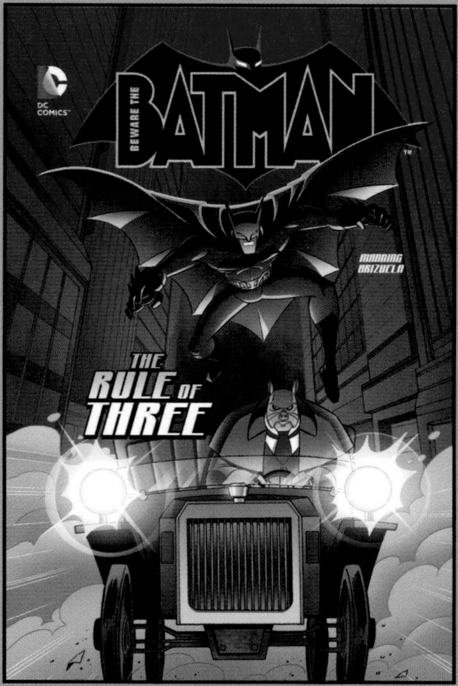
DC COMICS
BEWARE THE BATMAN
MANNING
BRIZUELA
THE RULE OF THREE

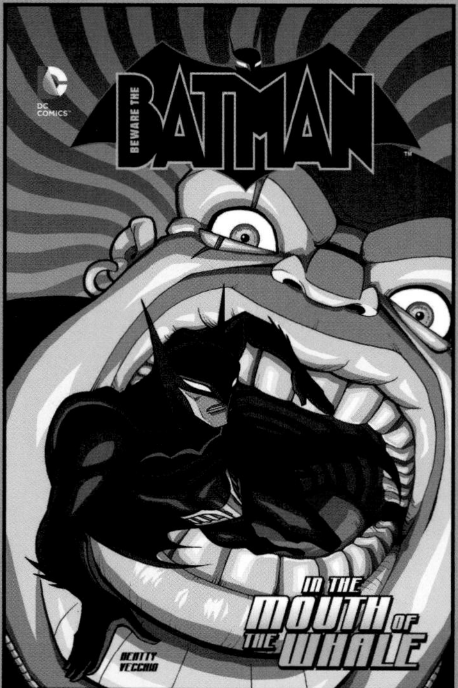
DC COMICS
BEWARE THE BATMAN
IN THE MOUTH OF THE WHALE
BEATTY
VECCHIO

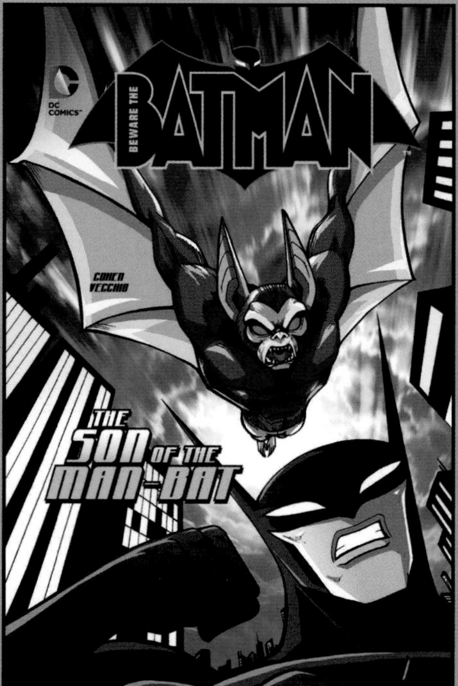
DC COMICS
BEWARE THE BATMAN
COHEN
VECCHIO
THE SON OF THE MAN-BAT

BEWARE THE BATMAN™

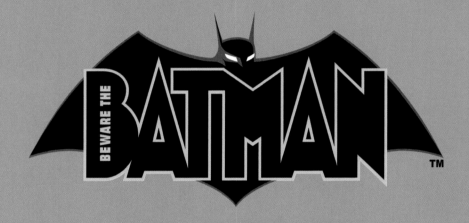